Angie Sage lives in
daughters aged sixt
studied illustration a
since then has illustr

D0538125

She started writing eleven years ago and ꞏꞏꞏ
writes and illustrates for ages three to ten. When
Angie Sage is not writing or drawing, she likes
sailing her boat, Muriel.

Angie Sage
Mouse

PUFFIN BOOKS

For the Brogs

PUFFIN BOOKS

Published by the Penguin Group
Penguin Books Ltd, 27 Wrights Lane, London W8 5TZ, England
Penguin Putnam Inc., 375 Hudson Street, New York, New York 10014, USA
Penguin Books Australia Ltd, Ringwood, Victoria, Australia
Penguin Books Canada Ltd, 10 Alcorn Avenue, Toronto, Ontario, Canada M4V 3B2
Penguin Books (NZ) Ltd, Private Bag 102902, NSMC, Auckland, New Zealand

On the World Wide Web at: www.penguin.com

Penguin Books Ltd, Registered Offices: Harmondsworth, Middlesex, England

First published 2001
1 3 5 7 9 10 8 6 4 2

Printed in Hong Kong by Midas Printing Ltd

British Library Cataloguing in Publication Data
A CIP catalogue record for this book is available from the British Library

ISBN 0–141–30949–0

Chapter One

"Why can't I come to school with you?" asked Mouse as she sat on the bed watching Izzy get ready for school.

"I don't know," Izzy said. "I wish you could. It would be much more fun if you were there."

"Time for breakfast!" Izzy's mum called up the stairs.

Izzy gave Mouse a big hug and a
kiss. "Got to go now or I'll be late.
Bye, Mouse!"

"Bye, Izzy," gasped Mouse, who felt
a bit squashed around the middle after
Izzy's hug. She gave Izzy a wave and
watched her disappear through the door.

Mouse had no idea what school was.
She thought it might be like a big shop
with things called teachers in, but what
she did know was that Izzy went there
every day and left her behind. Mouse
missed Izzy. She had been Izzy's
Mouse ever since she could remember.
When Izzy was little, Mouse used to

tell her stories at night when she couldn't sleep and Izzy had taken Mouse everywhere with her, even to playschool. But now it was different, Mouse was not allowed to go to school and the days without Izzy seemed very long.

So when Izzy was safely downstairs having her breakfast Mouse slipped out of bed. If Izzy wished that Mouse could go to school, thought Mouse, then

Mouse would go to school. Today.

Mouse scuttled across the bedroom carpet and into the bathroom. She swung herself up on to the washbasket and clambered on to the bathroom shelf by the mirror.

Mouse gazed at her reflection. She wanted to look smart for her first day at school. I wonder what colour I used to be? she thought as she looked at her fat, grubby tummy. Mouse took off her

old T-shirt and threw it on to the floor. She was a lot cleaner underneath.

"I shall have a BATH," decided Mouse. "Then I shall be the same colour all over."

Chapter Two

Have I ever had a bath? Mouse wondered as she looked down at the bath. It was very deep. Mouse was not sure if she could swim or not, so she decided to use the washbasin instead.

Mouse walked along the shelf to the washbasin and pulled hard on both taps. The water came rushing out. Mouse

grabbed hold of the bubble bath and
squeezed all of it into the basin. The
basin filled up and big floaty bubbles
began to drift around the bathroom.

Mouse stood on the edge of the
basin, held her nose and jumped in. The
water soaked into her and made her feel

heavy and kind of squashy, but Mouse
liked it. She could feel all the dirt float-
ing away while she splashed about in a
sea of bubbles.

There were lots of things Mouse
didn't know about baths and basins; one
of them was that you are meant to turn

off the taps when the basin is full. Luckily, one of the other things that Mouse did not know was that you are meant to put the plug in. But even so, the water was coming into the basin faster that it could go out, and it was not long before the bathroom floor was very wet and bubbly.

When Izzy came upstairs after breakfast to clean her teeth, her socks got wet. She slithered into the bathroom and turned off the taps.

"Mouse!" gasped Izzy, as she plunged her hand into the bubbly foam in the basin and pulled out a very heavy, dripping Mouse. Izzy's big sister, Jo, skidded into the bathroom a few moments later. Izzy quickly wrapped Mouse up in a towel.

"Look at the mess you've made," Jo said crossly. "What d'you want to go and wash your silly old Mouse for? It's time for school."

Jo mopped the floor with all the towels she could find while Izzy tried to dry out a wet, wriggling Mouse, who

was now a rather nice pale pink colour.

"Hurry up, you two!" Mum yelled up the stairs. "You'll be late for school."

"What shall I do with Mouse?" Izzy asked Jo. "I can't put her back to bed, she'll make it all wet."

"Stuff her in the airing cupboard," said Jo quickly. "She can get dry there." Jo opened the airing cupboard door and Izzy carefully put Mouse on top of a pile of towels.

"Bye, Mouse," said Izzy as she closed the airing cupboard door. "See you after school."

Mouse sat in the dark airing cupboard listening to Izzy and Jo going downstairs and off to school. Mouse was cross. There she was, all pink, clean and ready for school and Izzy was going without her.

Well, thought Mouse, we'll see about that. It will take more than being stuck in the airing cupboard to stop me going to school.

Mouse squished herself dry on the towels and then found a purple spotted T-shirt from a pile of baby clothes and put it on. It fitted perfectly. It wasn't quite like Izzy's school sweatshirt, but Mouse felt clean and smart in it. Then she slid down a pipe and landed on the airing cupboard floor. Mouse kicked the cupboard door hard. It flew open and Mouse fell out with a bump.

She sat on the floor at the top of the stairs and smiled. All she had to do now was to get to school.

··· Chapter Three ···

Jo and Izzy ran all the way to school.
They arrived puffed, but just in time.

"Oh no," said Izzy as they were
going in, "where's my lunch box?"

"On the kitchen table," said Jo, who
had just remembered the same thing.
"With my lunch box."

At that moment, Jo and Izzy's mum
was looking at two lunch boxes sitting

on the kitchen table.

"Oh no, they've forgotten their lunch boxes," she sighed. Mum wheeled her bike into the kitchen from the hall and went to find her coat and bicycle clips in the cupboard by the back door.

As she sifted through the pile of coats that had fallen on to the floor, there was a bumpety-bump sound as a slightly soggy Mouse made her way down the stairs and into the kitchen. The cupboard door slammed shut and

Mouse flattened herself against the wall, hoping that Mum hadn't seen her.

Mum hadn't. She stomped into the kitchen wearing her creased, muddy coat, which she had pulled out from underneath some wellingtons. Mouse crept around the corner and saw Mum hopping around in circles trying to put on her bicycle clips. The moment Mum turned her back, Mouse jumped into the bag on the back of the bike.

For once Mouse sat very quiet and still. She had to because as soon as she was in the bike bag Mum squashed two lunch boxes down on top of her. Then Mum closed the bag and pushed the bike down the garden path.

Mum's bike was not very new. It had bent old wheels and the handlebars

were difficult to keep straight. As Mum wobbled off down the lane to school, the bike swerved from side to side and hit all the bumps. Mouse began to feel sick.

Soon there were two sharp bends. "Eurgh ..." moaned Mouse.

Next a fast ride down the hill. "Aaargh!" squeaked Mouse.

And then the bike was bumped up on to the pavement outside the school. "OW!" yelled Mouse.

At last the lunch boxes were lifted out and Mum rushed into school with them. "Phew," breathed Mouse and stuck her head out of the bag. She saw Mum coming back so she quickly clambered out of the bag and jumped down. Mouse scuttled under a bush and watched Mum get back on the bike and wobble off down the road.

Then suddenly Mouse found herself flying through the air.

Chapter Four

A large teacher had scooped
Mouse up and was looking at
her carefully. Mouse looked back at the
teacher, but she knew better than to say
anything. Talking was only for people
who understood, like Izzy.

"Oh look," said the teacher, "a toy
anteater!"

Mouse let out a disgusted squeak.

"With a wonky squeaker." The teacher chuckled. "Well, come on, little anteater, let's take you to Lost Property. Someone's going to be missing you."

So Mouse was taken along to the school office and put on the Lost Property shelf.

Mouse liked sitting on the shelf. She had a good view of everything that was

going on and spent a very interesting
morning making faces when Mrs Jones,
the school secretary, wasn't looking and
waving at any children who came in
with messages. She kept hoping to see
Izzy come in but every time the door
opened it was someone else. Mouse
supposed it was Izzy's turn to come in
later on. School seemed a funny place

to Mouse. Try as she might, she could not work out what it was all for.

Just before lunch, Tom, who was a friend of Izzy's, came into the office.

"Miss Brent says please could you tell her what time we have to be in the hall for the puppet show?" Tom asked Mrs Jones.

Mrs Jones went to look in her diary. Mouse, who had been getting braver all morning, stood up on the shelf and did a little dance. She kicked her short legs up and down and flapped her arms around. She spun round, nearly fell off the shelf and sat down with a bump.

Tom opened his mouth and forgot to close it. He stared at Mouse as though he had seen a ghost.

"Half past two," said Mrs Jones. Tom

still had his mouth open. "Are you all
right, dear?" asked Mrs Jones. "You
look very pale."

Tom gave himself a little shake. "Oh.
Er, yes, thank you. I'm fine." Tom
walked out of the school office

backwards, still looking at Mouse.
Mouse stuck out her tongue and
waggled her ears as Tom slowly closed
the office door.

··· Chapter Five ···

Izzy ran into Tom in the playground. "Oof!"

"Sorry, Izz, didn't see you," said Tom, who had been wandering deep in thought.

"That's because you weren't looking."

"Yeah …" Tom gazed at Izzy as though deciding whether to say something or not. "Izzy …" he said.

"What?"

"Can anteaters stick out their tongues and wiggle their ears?" Tom asked slowly.

"Oh, I don't know that one. Well – can anteaters stick out their tongues and wiggle their ears?" said Izzy.

"It's not a joke," said Tom. "And it's not a real anteater either. A toy one."

"What, wiggling its ears and sticking out its tongue?" asked Izzy.

"Yep. And dancing and spinning round in circles. Just now. On the Lost

Property shelf." Tom thought Izzy might laugh at him. She usually did, but not this time.

"That's strange," she said. "What did it look like then, this anteater?"

"I'll show you," said Tom.

Izzy followed Tom round to the office window at the side of the school. The window was just too high up for Izzy, but Tom stood on tiptoe and peered in.

Mouse was still on the lost property shelf, but she was sitting quietly, gazing off into space. The office was closed at lunchtime and Mouse had no one to make faces at. She was also missing Izzy. Mouse was beginning to wonder how she was going to find Izzy in this school-place. When she had been stuck

in the bike bag underneath the lunch
boxes she had told herself that she
would spend a wonderful day with Izzy
doing all sorts of school-things (whatever they were). She had never dreamt
she would be sitting alone on a shelf all
day. Mouse sighed and saw Tom's face
peering in the window. It wasn't Izzy,
so she couldn't be bothered to wave this
time. Or even wiggle her ears.

Then suddenly it was Izzy! Mouse jumped up as Izzy's face hovered briefly outside the window. Izzy's eyes widened like two saucers as Mouse jumped up and waved. Then Izzy was gone.

"Oof!" gasped Tom. "You're heavy, Izz. Did you see the anteater then?"

"Er. Well, I didn't exactly see an anteater," said Izzy as Tom dropped her back to the ground.

"It was there, Izz. But it wasn't doing anything," Tom said, a little sadly. "But it did this morning, it danced and waggled its ears, honestly, Izz."

"Yes," said Izzy, "I'll bet it did."

Chapter Six

Suddenly the bell went. Lunchtime was over. Tom went off to the classroom, but Izzy rushed round to the school office and bumped into Mrs Jones.

Mrs Jones was with one of the strangest-looking people Izzy had ever seen. He had a pink bowler hat with bananas stuck all over it, purple

dungarees with green spots and a shirt made of luminous orange fur. Izzy almost forgot about Mouse when she saw him. Almost, but not quite.

"Mrs Jones, could I get something from Lost Property? Please!"

Mrs Jones looked a little flustered. It wasn't every day that someone wearing a pink bowler hat covered in bananas came to the school.

"No, Izzy," she said. "You know Lost Property can only be collected after school. Off you go now, you'll be late."

"But –" Izzy protested.

"After school, Izzy," said Mrs Jones, a little snappily. She pushed the man with bananas on his hat into the office and closed the door behind them.

Izzy went slowly back to her class,

wondering how Mouse could possibly have got herself on to the Lost Property shelf. By the time Izzy got back to the classroom, she was wondering whether it really was Mouse at all. Maybe she had imagined it. Maybe … or maybe not.

Chapter Seven

Back inside the school office, the man with bananas on his hat sat down.

"Let me get you a cup of tea, Professor Pootle," said Mrs Jones. "You look as though you could do with one." She bustled out to put the kettle on.

Professor Pootle stared at his spotty green knees in a particularly miserable way and muttered to himself.

"Oh, my poor puppets. All alone on the number nine bus. How could I forget them and leave them there? Whatever did they think when they saw me getting off the bus without them?"

Professor Pootle stood up and addressed the Lost Property shelf in a grand manner. He held out his arms and asked it, "And, pray tell me, how am I going to do a puppet show with no puppets?"

"Excuse me?" said a small squeaky voice.

Professor Pootle looked around, puzzled; hc had thought the room was empty. Mouse stood up in front of him and made a graceful bow.

"I am Mouse," she announced in her

loudest squeak. "The best dancer in the
world." Then she pointed her toes and
twirled along the Lost Property shelf.
"See?" she said proudly.

Professor Pootle stared at Mouse. He
was thinking fast.

"Can you do quick changes?" he
asked. "Can you sing, play the drums
and do headstands? Can you jump like

a rabbit and drive a digger?"

"Of course," said Mouse. "I do things like that all the time."

"You're hired!" said Professor Pootle.

··· Chapter Eight ···

By half past two the school hall was full and buzzing with talk as everybody waited for the puppet show to begin. Izzy's class was in the front row and Izzy sat right in front of the puppet theatre.

Professor Pootle stepped out in front of the small puppet theatre. He spread out his arms and said, "This *afternoon* it is *my pleasure* to introduce to you a *talented new star* who has stepped in at the *last moment* after a small, er … mishap."

Everyone clapped very loudly and Professor Pootle disappeared into the puppet theatre. The curtains drew back and a strange-shaped rabbit appeared.

"MOUSE!" yelled Izzy. Everyone
giggled.

"Sssh!" shushed Miss Brent. "It's a
rabbit, Izzy. Just settle down now."

Mouse had heard Izzy call out her
name. She swung round and her rabbit
ears fell off. Everyone laughed.

"It is a mouse," someone said.

"It's a fat mouse," someone else
giggled.

Mouse looked cross. She stuffed her

rabbit ears back on and waggled a cross
finger at the audience.

"I may be a mouse, but right now I
am a rabbit. This is a play about a
rabbit. So I am a rabbit. OK? And if
anyone else says I'm a mouse then they
can go away right now. Got that?"

The whole hall fell silent.

"Gosh. I could do with that mouse in my classroom," Miss Brent whispered to Mrs Jones.

"Did someone say something?" Mouse glared at Miss Brent. Miss Brent went pink.

"No? Good," said Mouse sternly.
"Then let the show begin, Professor!"

It was an amazing show. Mouse-the-
Rabbit was the hero. She had to stop
the diggers destroying the rabbits' field.
Mouse took all the parts. She saved the
field and rescued the smallest baby

rabbit from a bulldozer. At the end of the show, Mouse pranced on to the stage and took her bow. She pulled off her rabbit ears and threw them into the audience. Izzy caught them.

Chapter Nine

After school Izzy rushed round to the office. She knocked on the door and, to her surprise, Professor Pootle opened it.

"Oh," said Izzy, "is Mrs Jones here?"

"I believe the delightful Mrs Jones will return shortly," he said.

Izzy looked at the Lost Property shelf; there was no sign of Mouse. She

49

had an awful feeling that Professor
Pootle still had her.

"I've come to collect Mouse – I
mean some lost property," she said,
"but I can't see …"

"Here I am!" Mouse popped her head
out of Professor Pootle's dungaree
pocket.

"Oh, MOUSE!" gasped Izzy. "It's
home-time now. If you'd like to come

home, that is …"

"Of course I would. Help me out please, Professor," said Mouse.

"Your wish is my command, Miss Mouse." Professor Pootle lifted Mouse

out of his pocket and presented her to
Izzy.

"Oh, thank you, Professor," said Izzy.
She gave Mouse a big squeeze, just to
make sure it really was Mouse.

"No, thank *you*." He bowed. "I
understand my talented star lives
with you."

"Oh, er, yes, she does."

Professor Pootle smiled. "A rare talent," he said. "Of course, I asked Miss Mouse to tour with me, but she told me that you would be lost without her."

"Oh," said Izzy, surprised. "Well, I expect I would really."

"Ah indeed. And I understand only too well, because today I left my dearest puppets on the bus and –" Professor Pootle blew his nose loudly, "– and now I am lost without them."

"I'm sure they'll come back," said Mouse.

"Perhaps they will, Miss Mouse, perhaps they will." Professor Pootle picked up his banana-covered hat and walked to the office door. Then he turned and bowed a low bow.

"Goodbye, all!" he said.

"Goodbye, Professor!" squeaked Mouse as Professor Pootle strode off down the corridor.

Chapter Ten

Izzy walked home from school with Jo, as usual. Mouse, who was tired out after her performance, was curled up in Izzy's rucksack, fast asleep.

"That puppet show was good, wasn't it?" said Jo.

"Great," agreed Izzy.

"Couldn't see any strings, it was really clever. The rabbit looked a bit

like Mouse, though Mouse is fatter."
Jo laughed.

Izzy hoped Mouse was still fast
asleep. She didn't like being called fat.

"Hey, look!" said Izzy as the number
nine bus drove slowly past them. Sitting
on the back seat of the bus were five
puppets. Sitting next to them was a very
happy Professor Pootle. Izzy waved as

the bus disappeared into the distance and Professor Pootle and the puppets waved back.

"The puppets must have been on the bus all this time," said Jo.

When Izzy got home she gently took Mouse out of her rucksack and put her into bed. Mouse did not stir. Then Izzy took out the rabbit ears that she had caught at the puppet show and put them next to Mouse. In her sleep, Mouse's paw closed round them and held them tight.

Jo put her head round the door.

"What are you bringing tomorrow then?" she said.

"Bringing?" asked Izzy. "What? Where?"

"To school, silly. Last day of term you can bring a toy. What're you going to bring?"

Izzy didn't need to think about it. "Mouse," she said.

In her sleep, Mouse smiled.